Titles in Between The Lines:

Badger Publishing Limited, Oldmedow Road, Hardwick Industrial Estate, King's Lynn PE30 4JJ

Telephone: 01438 791037

www.badgerlearning.co.uk

ALONE

TIM COLLINS

Alone ISBN 978-1-78837-448-4

Publisher / Senior Editor: Danny Pearson
Editor: Claire Wood
Copyeditor: Cheryl Lanyon
Designer: Bigtop Design Ltd
Cover: © I. Glory / Alamy Stock Photo

2 4 6 8 10 9 7 5 3 1

CHAPTER 1
ALONE

Connor woke up and found himself alone in a silent house. He checked the bedrooms, the bathroom, the kitchen and the living room. There was no one anywhere.

"Jane?" he shouted. "Matt?"

He couldn't bring himself to call them Mum and Dad yet. Maybe he never would.

It didn't matter anyway. They weren't here.

He grabbed a bag of salt-and-vinegar crisps from the kitchen and ate them as he wandered around. Jane and Matt would never have let him do that. Crisps and chocolate were strictly for the evenings, and only if he'd been good and hadn't lost his temper all day.

But they weren't here now and he could do what he liked.

Connor glanced over at the patio door. A sheet of plywood covered the glass he'd broken the night before. He shouldn't have thrown the rock, but Jane and Matt shouldn't have told him he wasn't allowed a phone.

How was he meant to settle in and make friends at his new school if he didn't even have a phone?

Jane and Matt had been so angry that they'd sent him to his room. Then he'd heard Matt talking on the phone, then…

Then…?

He couldn't remember the rest of the night at all. He must have fallen asleep early.

He'd expected Jane and Matt to be waiting for him in the living room when he woke up, ready to lecture him.

Instead, he'd found the whole house empty. Had they given up and run away? He found himself grinning. Imagine what the foster agency would think when they found out. They'd sent him to the toughest parents they could find, and he'd broken them in less than a month.

But he knew that couldn't be right. It would take more than a smashed patio door to make Matt and Jane give up. Matt was tall and broad with a bald head and a bent nose, broken from playing rugby. He'd been in the army and he thought strictness and discipline could solve every problem. Connor had vowed to be the problem he could never solve.

Jane was small with short, grey hair and a face lined from scowling. She was always talking about how difficult things had been for her as a child and how much easier things were for kids now. Yeah, whatever. Nothing had been easy in Connor's life.

They were not the type to just give up. So where were they?

Connor wondered if they'd both died in a car crash. Maybe he'd be allowed to keep the house. Why not? He was almost old enough to live on his own. He could watch TV all night and throw epic parties. Everyone would want to be his friend if he had his own place.

He pulled open the blind on the living-room window. The car was still there. So much for that theory.

Once again, he wondered where Jane and Matt had got to. But then a bigger question popped into his mind — where was anyone?

It was Saturday morning. The kids from the house opposite should have been on their bikes. The old couple next door should have been working on their garden.

Park Street wasn't usually very busy, but it was never like this.

It was totally deserted. No cars, no bikes, no dog-walkers.

Connor grabbed his coat and stepped outside. He looked down the hill towards Station Road. It should have been blocked with cars heading for the supermarket by now. But it was also deserted.

He walked down the hill, peering into all the houses. There was no one moving around in any of them. Every house looked as empty as the one he'd just come from.

Connor reached Station Road. There was no one to be seen in either direction, and the traffic lights were switched off. He'd never seen that before.

There had been some sort of power cut. What did that have to do with everyone going missing?

The petrol station on the corner was totally dark. There was a large Solus logo above the shop and on all the pumps. Connor was sure it hadn't been there before. He recognised the word from somewhere, but he wasn't sure where.

He approached the door of the shop and gave it a shove. It wasn't locked.

"Hello?" he shouted.

There was no response.

He walked up to the aisle on the left of the till and grabbed a bag of chocolate raisins.

"I want to buy these," he said. "Can anyone help me?"

The whole place stayed silent. The power cut had taken out the fridges, and he could hear nothing but his own breathing.

"I'm going to take them without paying if no one comes," he said.

He shrugged. Did it still count as shoplifting when he'd gone to so much effort to find someone?

Probably. But it didn't matter. If the electricity was off, the CCTV cameras would be too.

Connor opened the bag and tossed a raisin into his mouth. He was still pretty full from the crisps, but he thought he might as well eat them. It wasn't every day you could get all the chocolate you wanted for free.

He stepped back onto Station Road, throwing the raisins into the air and catching some in his mouth.

A huge poster to his left featured the same Solus logo he'd seen on the petrol station. The words 'Treatment that gets results' were written underneath it.

Connor was done with the chocolate raisins. He was going to put the rest in his pocket, but he remembered he was on his own and could do whatever he liked.

He threw the raisins high into the air and watched them shower onto the road. A small sting of pain crept up his right arm. He didn't remember having hurt it recently.

Connor's thoughts turned back to his bizarre situation. Where had everyone gone? Had they been taken over by zombies? He'd seen lots of films where the human race is slowly turned into stinky walking corpses. Were some about to stagger around the corner and chomp on his brains?

No. Even if something like that were possible, there would be signs everywhere. Severed hands on the pavements. Puddles of blood on the roads. That sort of thing.

And if the human race had been wiped out by a deadly disease, there would be other types of evidence. The roads would be jammed with cars that were filled with corpses frozen in screams of pain.

But there was just nothing. It was as if everyone except him had been beamed into space.

If Matt and Jane had let him have a phone, he could at least try and contact someone. He'd told them he might need it in an emergency and they hadn't listened. Now look what had happened.

Connor realised he was heading for the Silvercross shopping centre. He hadn't meant to. It was just the way he always went.

He supposed it was as good a place as any. If anyone else had survived, they'd probably head there too.

He glanced up the road to his left. It was as deserted as all the others. No cars, no people, no lights.

Except there was something moving, halfway up the hill. In the driveway of one of the semi-detached houses, a green recycling bin was rattling around.

Maybe it was just the wind, but maybe someone was shaking it from the other side. Someone who could tell him what was going on.

"Hey!" he yelled. "Is anyone there?"

There was no reply.

Connor strode up the hill. If they were hiding from him, he'd make them regret it.

CHAPTER 2

THE SHOPPING CENTRE

The bin rumbled as Connor approached. He walked slowly with his hands out, ready to grab whoever was there.

He stepped around the bin. A black cat was scraping its claws on the side, making thin lines in the green plastic. It saw him and fled around the side of the house.

Connor slumped his shoulders. It finally hit him. He was alone. Every time he thought he saw someone, it would turn out to be another cat, or a dog, or a squirrel. There would be no humans around to tell him what had happened. He'd never know.

He kicked the bin over and watched as cans and bottles rolled onto the drive. A spark of pain shot up his leg, just like the one he'd felt in his arm when he'd thrown the raisins. That was odd. But so were lots of things right now.

He trudged back down the hill, aware that there were tears in his eyes and glad that no one was around to see them.

He was used to loneliness. It was a feeling he went through every time he had to move to a new home and a new school. But at least there had always been the possibility he'd find someone he'd connect with. Now there was nothing, no one, and there never would be.

He'd even take the company of his foster parents right now. Matt's stories about the army would be better than this horrible silence. And Jane's lectures about feeding a whole family on five pounds a week would be preferable too.

Connor told himself to keep going. He didn't know for sure that he was alone. There could be someone, or a whole bunch of people, waiting in the shopping centre.

He spotted a newsagent to his right. The lights were off, as they were in every shop, but the door was open.

He strolled in and looked at the row of newspapers. None of them gave any clues about what had happened. There was nothing about a national emergency or a scary new disease that would wipe everyone out.

The word Solus was on every front page. The same word Connor had seen on the petrol station and on the poster.

Connor grabbed one of the papers and read the story. It turned out that Solus was the name of a new treatment for criminals and troublemakers. It promised to cure them in a matter of days. That it was all 'for the greater good'. Some people thought it was a perfect way to cure bad people. Some thought it was too harsh. Connor didn't really care. He just wanted to know what had happened to everyone.

Connor tossed the newspaper over his shoulder. There was another jolt of pain in his arm.

He grabbed a box of chocolates on his way out. He tore away the plastic wrapper and opened the lid as he walked.

There were pictures inside showing which chocolates were which. Connor popped a caramel swirl into his mouth and threw an orange cream at the window of a tanning shop. Pain jolted up his arm again.

A strange idea came into Connor's mind. Someone was making him feel the pain. It happened whenever he threw stuff. It was impossible, of course. But just in case it was true, Connor decided to try something.

He bent down and pulled up the broken corner of a paving stone. He tossed it in the air and caught it a couple of times, getting a feel for its weight. Then he drew it back. There was already a tingling in his arm.

He threw it at the tanning shop window. It bounced off, but managed to crack the glass, creating a jagged, white spider-web pattern.

There wasn't just pain this time. There was agony. The muscles in Connor's right arm tensed and cramped. He winced and rubbed them, with tears streaming down his face.

For a moment he thought he was going to die right there in front of the tanning shop, with no one to hear him as he shouted for help.

But the feeling eventually went away.

Connor told himself to stop worrying about the pain and get to the shopping centre.

At the end of Station Road he turned into Mill Lane, a short road that only buses were allowed on. There was nothing on it at all today except for some pigeons and a crisp packet.

The huge grey block of the Silvercross Centre was ahead. Except it wasn't called the Silvercross Centre any more. It had the Solus logo on the side, just like the petrol station.

There was something else Connor couldn't make sense of. According to the newspaper, it was the name of a treatment for criminals. So why was it written on everything? Some sort of publicity stunt, maybe.

Connor strolled into the dark shopping centre. It was so strange to see the huge space without any lights on. It was usually so bright. And it was always full of noise too, with all the background music, chatter and screaming children.

"Hello?" shouted Connor. "Is anyone here?"

He heard nothing but his own voice echoing off the walls.

"If you're in here, let me know!" he yelled.

He walked past the dark shops, heading for the food court on the top floor. Surely that would be the place any survivors would gather.

He trudged up the frozen escalators, shouting "Hello!" over and over again. If there was anyone there, he didn't want to take them by surprise. Especially if they were as freaked out by everything as he was.

He reached the top floor. It was lighter up here. To his left was a wide corridor lined with shops. Ahead was the food court, with two rows of stalls either side of a large cluster of tables and chairs. Beyond them was a huge window that stretched from floor to ceiling.

Connor sighed. There was no one here. No one to tell him what had happened. No one to explain about the pain. No one to tell him what Solus had to do with anything.

He stepped up to the massive window and looked out over the town. The square below had been taken over by pigeons now all the shoppers had gone. Beyond it he could see roads, houses, churches, parks, and a steep hill in the distance with a square, white building on top.

He had been stupid to think anyone would be here to help him. He'd been left behind by everyone, just like he always was.

He could feel his pulse speeding and his muscles tightening. Thoughts were racing through his mind and he needed to do something to silence them. He dug his nails into his palms until it felt like the skin would break. It wasn't enough. He needed to do something big.

This is what it had felt like before he'd broken Matt and Jane's patio door, and before all the other bad things he'd done.

This time there was no one around to stop him doing some real damage. He dragged a chair over to the window and lifted it above his head. He'd show everyone what he thought about being abandoned.

He was about to slam it into the glass when the pain came back. It was a hot, buzzing feeling that filled his body and zapped his strength. He dropped the chair and collapsed to the floor.

Connor couldn't move. He couldn't stop his muscles shaking and he couldn't stop the tears from running down his cheeks.

CHAPTER 3
BREAKING GLASS

Connor got his breath back and pushed himself to his feet. His muscles were still aching, but at least he could move.

He staggered over to one of the fridges and pulled out a bottle of water.

As he drank it, he thought again about how Matt and Jane had said he didn't need a phone. If he ever saw them again, he'd let them know how wrong they'd been.

Something occurred to Connor and he got angry with himself for not thinking of it sooner.

There was a phone shop just a few metres away. Nobody owned any of them any more. They were all his for the taking.

He slammed the water down onto a table and strode out into the corridor. It got darker as he went away from the big window, but he could still make out the different shopfronts.

The phone shop was on the right. Inside were long white tables covered with small black rectangles. He tried to grab the first one on the first table, but it was stuck to a display stand.

He bent over it and felt around the sides until he found a button. Bright white light shone into his face, making him squint.

The words NO SIM were written in the top-left corner of the screen.

He went along the tables, switching all the phones on. Surely one of them must have a sim card?

The shop got lighter as he filled the room with glowing rectangles.

Eventually he reached the last phone. It didn't work either. He felt like finding something to smash them all with.

The first phones were turning themselves off again now. Soon he'd be alone in the dark with thousands of pounds worth of useless technology.

Connor looked around the room in the fading light to see if he'd missed anything. A wall-mounted display of covers, a bin of chargers, a flat white counter at the back of the room.

There was another phone on the counter. This one wasn't stuck to a stand. Maybe someone had been in the middle of using it when everyone disappeared.

Connor ran for it and reached it just as the final phones were going dark. He switched it on. This one didn't say NO SIM. It said SEARCHING...

Connor raced out of the shop, waving the handset ahead of him to try and get a signal. He rushed along the top level of the shopping centre, accidentally bumping into the side of a smoothie stall. He didn't care. He just wanted to be able to contact someone.

The word SEARCHING... remained on the screen.

He reached the food court and went back to the large window. If he could get a signal anywhere, it would be here.

He span around, keeping his eyes on the screen. Still nothing but SEARCHING...

Connor crouched down and put the phone near the floor.

SEARCHING...

Connor stood on a chair and lifted the phone high into the air.

SEARCHING…

His heart sank. It wasn't going to work. Whatever had taken out the power had taken out the entire phone network too. He was stupid for ever thinking he had a hope.

He threw the phone at the window. It bounced off and smashed down on the floor with a pleasing crack. A jolt of pain swept up his right arm again.

Why did this keep happening? It was like his own body was trying to stop him breaking stuff. He wasn't going to let it.

Connor picked up the chair he'd tried to smash the window with before. He was going to have another go. And this time he wasn't going to stop until he'd succeeded.

Pain was coming. But he was prepared for it. He'd work through it until he'd broken the window.

He bit down on his lip and slammed the chair into the glass, making a thin crack. Agony flooded his muscles. He ignored it and hit the glass again.

The crack widened on either side. It felt like a hundred needles were jabbing into his arms and chest, but Connor told himself not to give up. He gripped the chair with his trembling hands and struck the glass again.

This time it worked. A huge section of the window caved outwards and smashed onto the ground far below. Cold wind blew in through the jagged hole.

The effort of fighting the pain had exhausted Connor, but it had been worth it. He found himself smiling as he collapsed to the floor.

He had beaten the pain. He had won.

*

When he woke up it was night. His arms ached, his mouth was dry and his head was throbbing. He got to his feet and picked up his bottle of water.

He took a swig and gazed out at the dark town.

By the light of the moon he could see narrow streets, some with cats and dogs patrolling them; abandoned market stalls; bus shelters with their displays turned off; and dark shops with their doors open.

Connor gasped.

There was something strange in the distance. On the top floor of the white building on the hill there was a light on.

Connor was vaguely aware that he'd dropped his bottle of water and it was spilling around his feet.

Maybe the white building hadn't been touched by the power cut while everything around it had. But it was much more likely that someone was inside that room.

He had to reach them before they went away. He raced back to the escalators.

CHAPTER 4

THE TREATMENT ROOM

Connor climbed the hill with his eyes fixed on the white building. The light was still on in the room at the top.

There was a tall, metal fence in front of him and he leant against it to get his breath back. Getting here from the town centre had taken over two hours, even though he'd run most of the way.

He'd been terrified the light would go out and he'd miss whoever was in there forever.

He followed the fence until he came to an empty booth and a barrier to stop cars. The Solus logo was printed on the side. Maybe the person in the room could tell him why he kept seeing it.

He ducked under the barrier and approached a set of automatic glass doors. He stepped in front of them, wondering if the power was on for the whole building or just the room at the top.

They didn't budge. Connor shoved his fingertips into the small space between the doors and tried to drag them apart. They moved a few inches with a horrible screeching noise.

He hadn't made much of a gap, but it was just about wide enough to squeeze through.

Inside was a dingy reception area with a desk on the left and a white leather sofa on the right. Connor stepped slowly across the polished floor. He kept expecting a burglar alarm to ring out, but he heard nothing except the squeaking of his shoes.

There were four lifts beyond the reception, but he wasn't even going to try those. The last thing he wanted was to get stuck between floors and slowly starve to death. He walked past the lifts and shoved open the door to the stairwell.

He stepped inside and let the door close behind him. He was in complete darkness now. There were no windows for the moonlight to seep through.

He wished he hadn't thrown the phone away. It would have made a very useful torch.

Connor climbed slowly, gripping the handrail.

He imagined the mysterious person from the top floor racing down to attack him and he found his hands trembling. Maybe they'd think he was here to steal from them. Maybe they didn't want a guest in any case.

He told himself to stop imagining things. He had to know why the room on the top floor was the only place in the whole of the town with a light on. There was no point in freaking himself out before he got there.

He climbed up six flights in silence and darkness. Finally, the handrail came to an end. He reached out and felt the outline of a door. He pushed it open and stepped into a corridor with a dim glow coming from the right.

"Hello?" he shouted. "Is anyone there?"

He crept towards the light. This was it. The room he'd seen from the top of the shopping centre. The room where he'd finally get some answers.

A small window in the door was throwing a bright strip of light on the wall opposite. The words Treatment Room 4 were etched on a metal sign.

"Hello?" he shouted again.

He could hear nothing coming from inside the room but a low electrical humming.

Connor peered through the small window. He could see green walls lined with shelves that housed messy stacks of papers and notebooks, but there was no sign of any people.

He knocked on the door. There was no reply.

He opened the door very slowly. It was so much brighter than the rest of the building that his eyes took a moment to adjust.

There was a narrow single bed with a green plastic sheet in the middle of the room. It was covered with wires that trailed to a table with three chunky laptops on. A black piece of plastic was resting on top of the bed. It looked like a stand for the sort of headset that might be used for a computer game.

Behind the table were two chairs, both of which had pencils and notepads on.

Connor stepped over and examined the laptops. All three of them were on, running some sort of program that showed a diagram of a human brain with certain areas glowing red and yellow.

A sign hung on the wall above. It read 'Solus — For the greater good'. Connor turned to the other side of the room. On the windowsill next to one of the chairs was a coffee cup with the Solus logo on. Connor placed his hands around it. It was still warm.

This was good. Whoever was using this room had been here very recently. Connor thought about going out into the corridors and looking for them, but he decided to stay where he was. They were hardly going to abandon all this equipment. They'd be back soon.

He figured he might as well lie on the bed while he was waiting. The journey from the shopping centre had been exhausting, but it had all been worth it. He'd found a room that was still being used. He was about to meet whoever was using it.

Connor felt his eyes drooping shut. He told himself to stay awake. The room's owner would get a shock if they came back and found him asleep.

But he was so tired. Maybe a small nap wouldn't be so bad.

*

Connor woke up. There were voices all around him. Someone was lifting something heavy from his head.

He was in a bright room, surrounded by people. A man with a grey moustache was standing on his left and scribbling into a notepad. A woman with thick-rimmed glasses was on his right, holding a black-plastic headset. That must have been the thing that was on his head.

In the two chairs behind the laptops were Jane and Matt, his so-called mum and dad. Jane was scowling and shaking her head, while Matt was grinning and holding the Solus coffee cup.

"Oh dear," said Matt. "You didn't do very well, did you?"

CHAPTER 5
SOLUS

Connor's legs were strapped to the bed. There were wires attached to his fingers and chest.

"Where were you all?" he asked.

"Here," said Jane. She pointed at one of the laptop screens. "Watching you in the simulation."

Connor tried to sit up. One of the wires fell away from his chest and the woman with the thick-rimmed glasses tutted, pushed him down and stuck it back on again.

"Please don't disrupt the equipment," she said. "It will only mean we're all here longer."

"I looked all over town for you," said Connor. "I couldn't see anyone at all."

Matt laughed so much he spat some of his coffee out.

"That proves the program works," said Matt. "He still thinks it was all real."

"It takes a few moments for the memory to return," said the man with the grey moustache. "It's perfectly normal."

Connor had no idea what the man was talking about. He could remember everything. Waking up in the empty house, going to the shopping centre, trying to make the phone work, smashing the window, seeing the light in the distance.

But then these things began to fade from his mind. It seemed like they'd happened years rather than hours ago.

A new set of memories replaced them. Matt and Jane discovering the broken patio door. Matt yelling at him until his face was red and the veins in his neck were bulging. Jane suggesting that they try to cure him using the Solus technique. Driving to the white building on the hill, the headquarters of the Solus company.

Connor had been shown into this treatment room by the woman with the thick-rimmed glasses. She'd strapped him to the bed and stuck the wires onto him while the man with the grey moustache had injected green fluid into his arm.

The woman had fixed the headset on and explained that he was about to enter a simulation. He would find himself in a very frustrating situation, but he mustn't react with anger. If he did, he'd be punished with electric shocks.

He'd wanted to tell her he wouldn't take part in her stupid simulation and that he was going home. But instead he'd fallen into a deep sleep.

Then he'd woken up in the empty house. Except he hadn't. None of that had really happened. It had all been part of this stupid Solus thing.

Connor struggled against his straps and tried to rip the wires out of his chest.

"Get me off this bed!" he yelled. "I didn't agree to this!"

The woman with the thick-rimmed glasses held him down while the man with the grey moustache injected a syringe of green fluid into his arm.

"Stop it," Connor said. He tried to shout it, but it came out as no more than a whisper. The strength was draining out of him. He needed to sleep.

"So what happens now?" asked Jane.

"We run the test again," said the woman with the thick-rimmed glasses.

Everything went dark. Connor wanted to thrash his head around, but he couldn't move.

"And we increase the levels of the shocks," said the man with the grey moustache. "With your permission, of course."

"Go for it," said Matt. "Give him whatever he needs. We know that this is for the best. For the greater good."

"The greater good," repeated Jane.

Connor wanted to promise never to break anything again if they'd take the headset and the wires off. He wouldn't be able to stand it all again. Not the pain, not the loneliness. But he was too weak even to move his lips.

*

Connor woke up and found himself alone in a silent house.

THE END

ABOUT THE AUTHOR

Tim Collins is originally from Manchester, and now lives near Oxford. He has written more than 90 books, including *Wimpy Vampire*, *Cosmic Colin* and the Long-Lost Secret Diary of the World's Worst series. He has won awards in the UK and Germany.